MARISABINA RUSSO

Trade-in Mother

GREENWILLOW BOOKS
New York

**For Whitney
and for our children,
Hannah, Sam, and Ben**

Gouache paints were used
for the full-color art.
The text type is Korinna.
Copyright © 1993 by
Marisabina Russo Stark

Greenwillow Books,
a division of William Morrow
& Company, Inc.,
1350 Avenue of the Americas,
New York, NY 10019.

Printed in Hong Kong
by South China Printing
Company (1988) Ltd.
First Edition
10 9 8 7 6 5 4 3 2 1

Library of Congress
Cataloging-in-Publication Data

Russo, Marisabina.
Trade-in mother /
by Marisabina Russo
    p.   cm.
Summary: Max discusses
with his mother good
reasons why he'd like
to trade her in,
but admits there is
one reason to keep her.
ISBN 0-688-11416-4 (trade).
ISBN 0-688-11417-2 (lib.)
[1. Mothers and sons—Fiction.]
I. Title.
PZ7.R9192Tr   1993
[E]—dc20
91-47681   CIP   AC

Max wanted to wear his favorite shirt to school.
"No, it's too dirty," said Mama. "I'm going to wash it today."
"Rats," said Max.

Max wanted Chunky O's for breakfast.
"Looks like the box is empty," said Mama.
"Thanks a lot," said Max.

Max did not want to wear his jacket to school. It was sunny and bright.
"It's very chilly," said Mama. "Wear your jacket."
"No way!" said Max. But he did.

When Max came home from school, he wanted to ride his bike.
"We have to take your sister to her Girl Scout meeting," said Mama.

"Why can't I just stay home?" said Max. "I'm not a Girl Scout."
"Because you're too little to stay home by yourself," said Mama.

Before dinner Max wanted to have a couple of cookies, just to tide him over.

"No," said Mama. "You can wait until dessert to have your cookies."

"You're the meanest mother in the whole world," said Max.

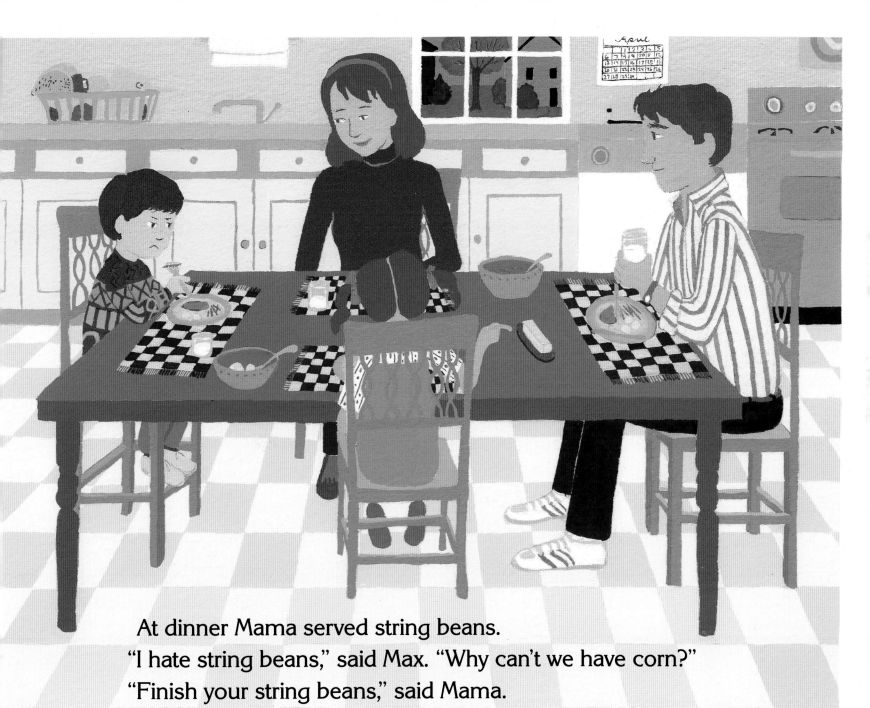

At dinner Mama served string beans.
"I hate string beans," said Max. "Why can't we have corn?"
"Finish your string beans," said Mama.

After dinner Max took a bath. He played with his boats
and sponges.
Then Mama came in and took down the shampoo.
"You're not going to wash my hair, are you?" said Max.
"Yes, I am," said Mama.
"Nothing is going right today," said Max.

At bedtime Mama read a book about pirates.
It was Max's favorite book.
When she was done, he said, "Please read it again."
"No, it's too late," said Mama. "You have school tomorrow."

"You are definitely the worst mother in the whole world,"
 said Max. "I wish I could trade you in!"
"Where would you trade me in?" asked Mama.

"At this special store," said Max. "A store where they have all these other mothers to choose from. All these nicer, better mothers."

"I don't think I want to be traded in," said Mama.
"I would miss you too much. May I have a kiss good-night?"
"No," said Max.
"What kind of mother would you trade me in for?" asked Mama.

"I would trade you in for a mother who lets me wear
dirty shirts," said Max.

"I would trade you in for a mother who buys truckloads
of Chunky O's and never forgets."

"I would trade you in for a mother who lets me go out
without a jacket even when it's snowing."

"I would trade you in for a mother who lets me stay home all by myself."

"I would trade you in for a mother who lets me eat cookies whenever I want to."

"I would trade you in for a mother who hates
string beans as much as I do."

"I would trade you in for a mother
who never washes my hair."

"I would trade you in for a mother who reads me my
favorite book at least ten hundred times each night."

"I would trade you in for a mother
who doesn't kiss me good-night."

"I would never trade you in," said Mama.

"Is there really a place to trade in
little boys?" asked Max.

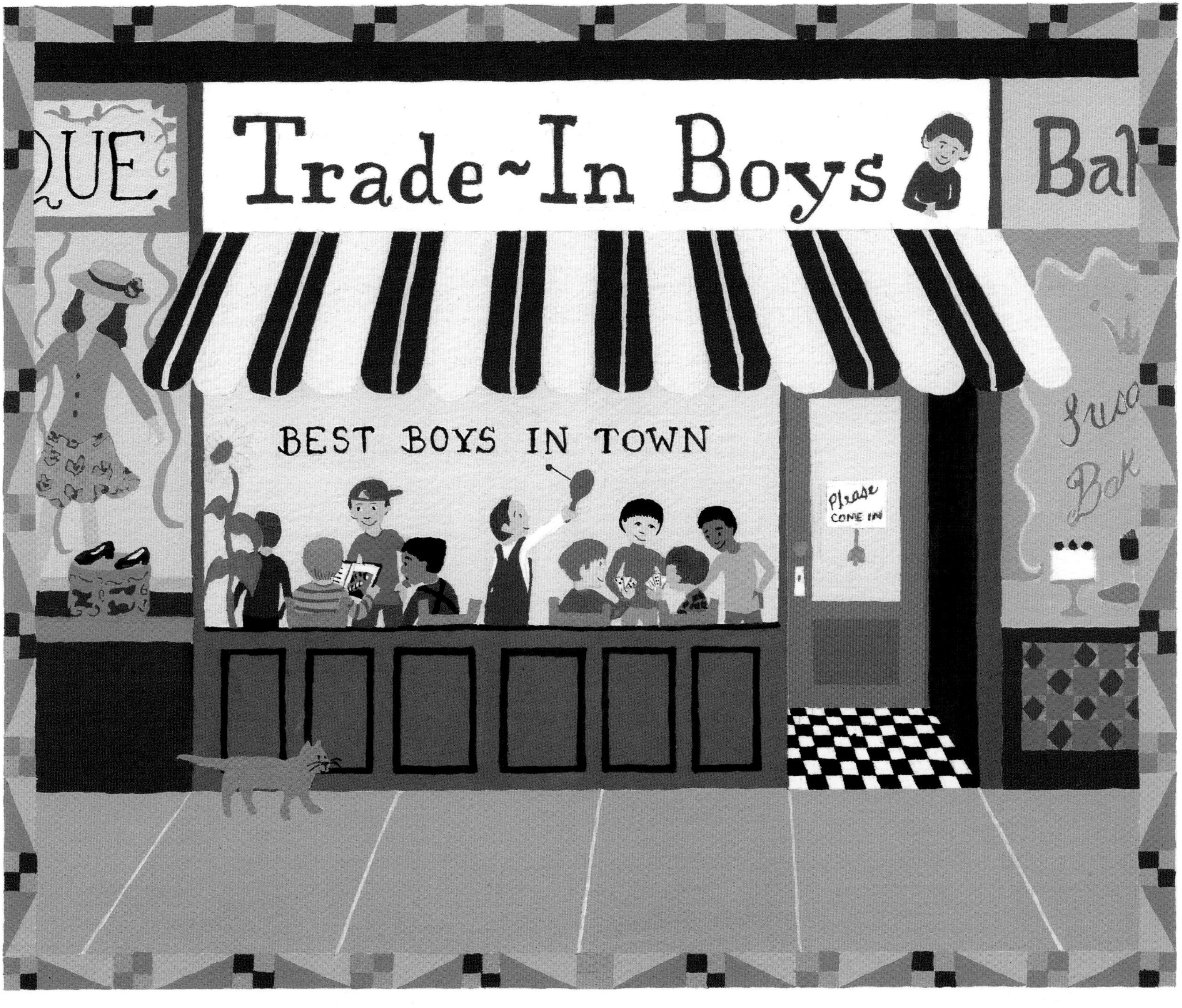
QUE
Trade~In Boys
Bak
BEST BOYS IN TOWN
Please
COME IN

"No," said Mama.

"That's good," said Max. "Don't worry, Mama.
 I'm not going to trade you in.
 I'll give you another chance."

"Thank you," said Mama.

"Anyway, I don't really want a mother who
 doesn't kiss me good-night," said Max.

"I'm glad," said Mama, and she gave Max a kiss.
"Good-night," said Max.